To Sir Tomás
–R.A.–

To Sir Adam
–A.R.–

ORCHARD BOOKS
338 Euston Road, London, NW1 3BH
Orchard Books Australia
Level 17/207 Kent Street,
Sydney, NSW 2000
First published in 2007 by Orchard Books
ISBN: 978 1 84616 376 0

A CIP catalogue record for this book is available from the British Library.
10 9 8 7 6 5 4 3 2 1
Designed by David Mackintosh
Printed in Singapore
Orchard Books is a division of Hachette Children's Books

Written by Ronda Armitage
Illustrated by Arthur Robins

SMALL Knight lived in a cold, old castle on a spiky, high hill. He didn't mind that it was cold or old. He loved the castle so much that he never wanted to go anywhere else.

ONE morning, Dad Knight announced that it was time for Small Knight to have his first suit of armour
and his first horse
and his first shield
and his first sword
and to go out to fight
his first fierce dragon.

Small Knight didn't want to fight a dragon. He wanted to play kick-a-ball with his friends. He didn't even know what a dragon looked like.

"DRAGONS live in caves,
they breathe fire and they're
very fierce," explained Dad Knight.
"You'll know one when you see one.
Knights have to be big and brave and
fight them. That's what knights do."

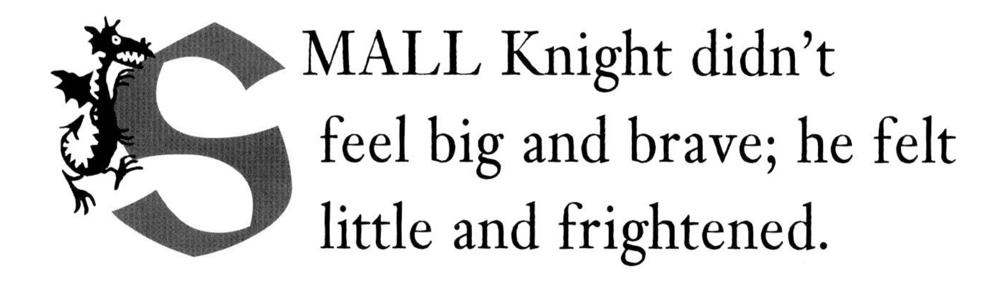

SMALL Knight didn't feel big and brave; he felt little and frightened.

He clunked in his armour and shivered in his boots, and made up a song as he rode along:

"This is a tale of
a big brave knight
Who one fine day
went out to fight
A very fierce dragon
who lived in a cave."

5

SOON Small Knight came to a hovel. He tapped on the door. "I'm looking for a very fierce dragon," he said politely. "Have you seen one about?"

"Don't talk to me about
fierce dragons," said Mr Peasant.
"One knocked the roof off my
hovel with a swipe of its scaly tail.
Are you sure you want to fight
a very fierce dragon?"
"It's what brave knights do,"
explained Small Knight.

But he looked at the hovel
and he didn't feel brave.

SMALL Knight came to a village. Six damsels were brushing their golden hair. "Excuse me," called Small Knight. "I'm looking for a very fierce dragon. Have you seen one about?"

"Don't talk to us about fierce dragons," cried the six damsels. "One roared down the street this morning. He gave us such a fright he made our hair stand on end. Are you sure you want to fight a very fierce dragon?"
"It's what brave knights do," explained Small Knight.

But he gazed at their hair and he didn't feel brave.

SMALL Knight came to a forest. A woodcutter was sitting on a tree stump.

"Good afternoon," said Small Knight. "I'm looking for a very fierce dragon. Have you seen one about?"

"Don't talk to me about fierce dragons," groaned the woodcutter. "One breathed fire and burnt the forest down. Are you sure you want to fight a very fierce dragon?"
"It's what brave knights do," explained Small Knight.

But he looked at the trees and he didn't feel brave.

SMALL Knight clunked in his armour and shivered in his boots. He sang a different song as he rode along:

"This is a song of
a not-so-brave knight
Who decided one day
he didn't want to fight
A very fierce dragon
who lived in a cave."

ON the way home he found a little creature. "Good evening," said Small Knight. "I'm Small Knight, and I'm *supposed* to be looking for a very fierce dragon. Have you seen one about?"

"Don't talk to me about fierce dragons," cried the little creature. "I used to have a lovely dark home in a hill, but some very fierce dragons moved in, and now I have no home. Are you sure you want to fight a very fierce dragon?"

"NOT now," said Small Knight. "It's getting dark. I'll look for a very fierce dragon tomorrow. Please don't cry. You can stay at my home tonight."

"Thank you, Small Knight," sniffled the little creature. "Please call me George."

So, Small Knight and George hurried home.

Mum and Dad Knight were
waiting on the drawbridge.

"Hello, Mum," called Small Knight.
"I've brought my new friend home
to stay."

MUM Knight and the ladies-in-waiting all screamed.

Everyone scrambled up to the Minstrels' Gallery.

"Mum, Dad,"

called Small Knight.

"I've been looking for dragons to fight all day and now it's time for tea."

"You only had to fight
the very fierce dragon . . ."

called Mum Knight.

"You didn't have to
bring him home!"

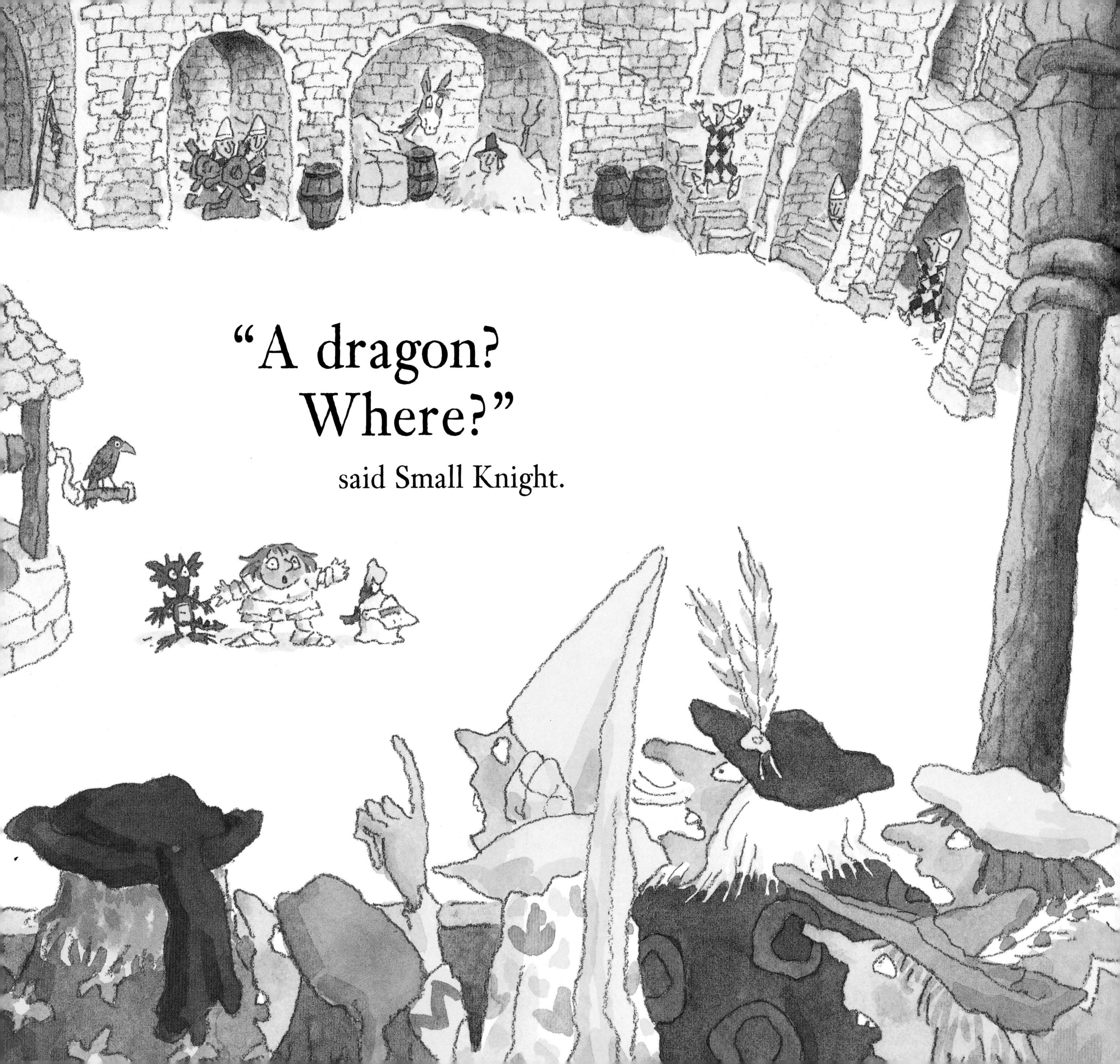

“A dragon?
Where?”

said Small Knight.

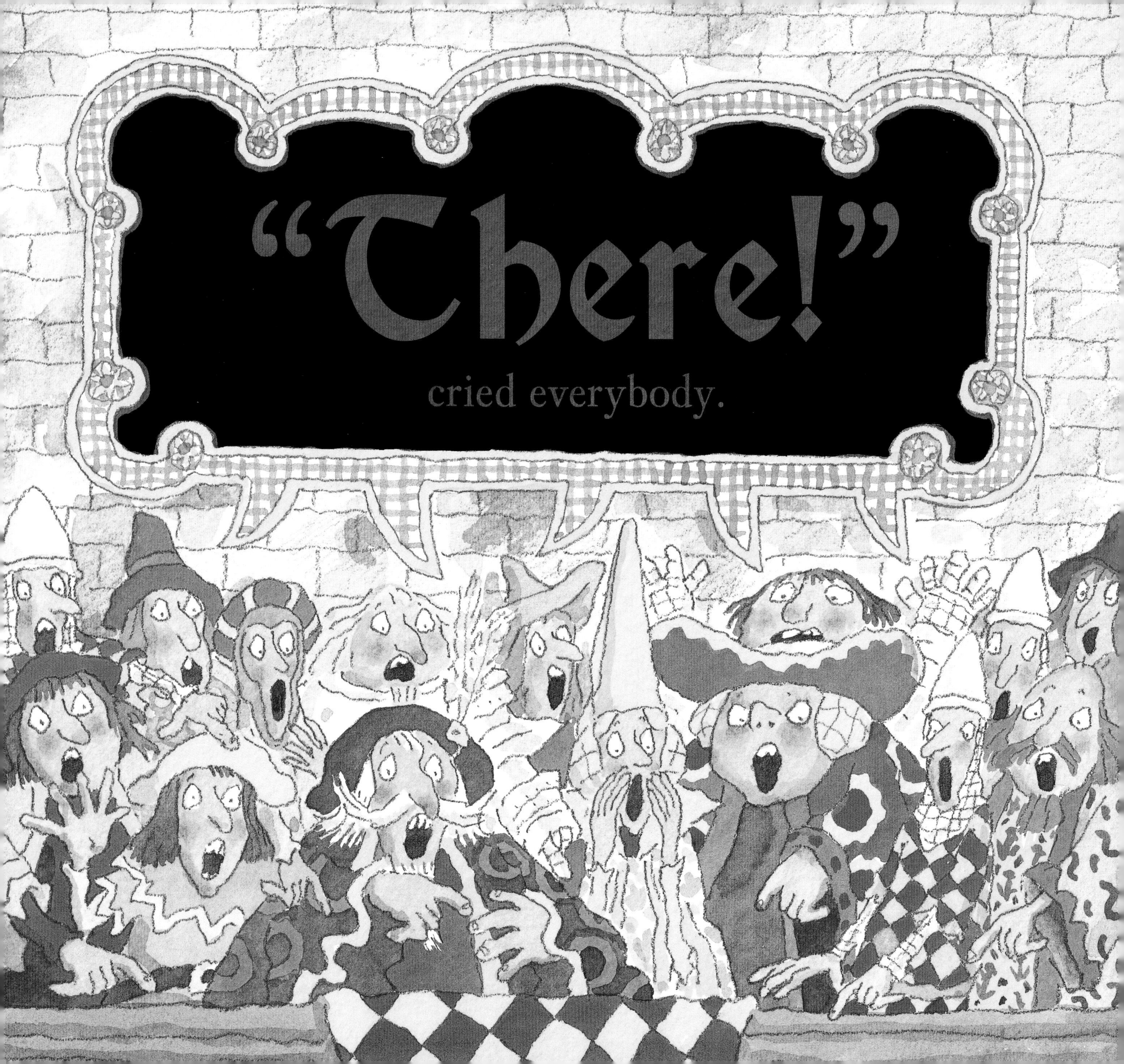
"There!"
cried everybody.

“Get behind me, George,” shouted Small Knight. “There’s a very fierce dragon about. I’m a big brave knight; I’ll look after you.”

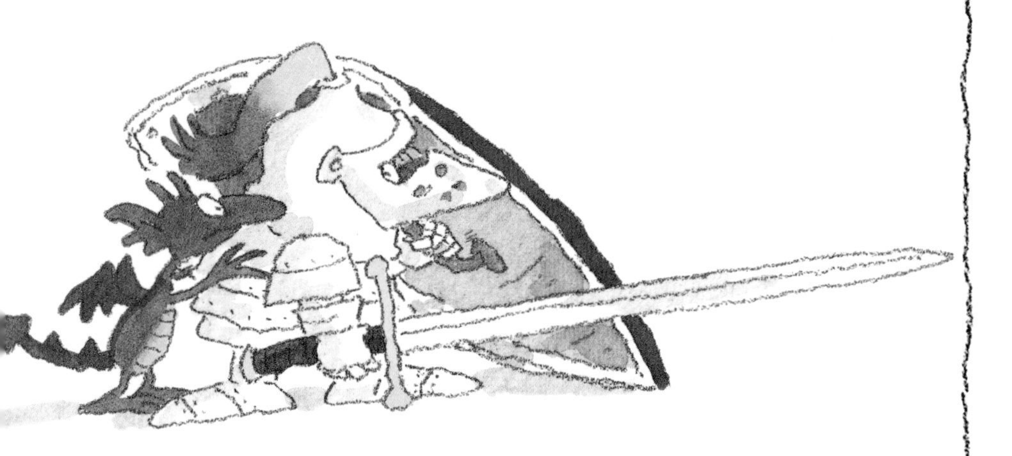

“Excuse me, Small Knight,” said George. “I think there’s been a mistake. I’m the dragon.”

“But dragons are big and fierce and breathe fire,” said Small Knight.

“I’m a small, friendly sort of dragon,” smiled George. “I’m frightened of fierce dragons too.”

“A dragon!” cheered Small Knight. “A real dragon. Could you pretend to be very fierce so I can fight you?”

NEXT morning, they had a wonderful fight where no one won at all, and they played kick-a-ball for the rest of the day.

Everybody loved George.

He showed all the knights the best way to fight very fierce dragons. And he learned to breathe fire to keep that cold, old castle warm . . .

And as for Small Knight and George?

Well, they were the very best of friends, and Small Knight never had to fight a very fierce dragon again.